Dear Parents:

Congratulations! Your child is taking the first steps on an exciting journey. The destination? Independent reading!

STEP INTO READING® will help your child get there. The program offers five steps to reading success. Each step includes fun stories and colorful art or photographs. In addition to original fiction and books with favorite characters, there are Step into Reading Non-Fiction Readers, Phonics Readers and Boxed Sets, Sticker Readers, and Comic Readers—a complete literacy program with something to interest every child.

Learning to Read, Step by Step!

Ready to Read   Preschool–Kindergarten
• big type and easy words • rhyme and rhythm • picture clues
For children who know the alphabet and are eager to begin reading.

Reading with Help   Preschool–Grade 1
• basic vocabulary • short sentences • simple stories
For children who recognize familiar words and sound out new words with help.

Reading on Your Own   Grades 1–3
• engaging characters • easy-to-follow plots • popular topics
For children who are ready to read on their own.

Reading Paragraphs   Grades 2–3
• challenging vocabulary • short paragraphs • exciting stories
For newly independent readers who read simple sentences with confidence.

Ready for Chapters   Grades 2–4
• chapters • longer paragraphs • full-color art
For children who want to take the plunge into chapter books but still like colorful pictures.

STEP INTO READING® is designed to give every child a successful reading experience. The grade levels are only guides; children will progress through the steps at their own speed, developing confidence in their reading.

Remember, a lifetime love of reading starts with a single step!

Step into Reading, Random House, and the Random House colophon are registered trademarks of Penguin Random House LLC.

Visit us on the Web!
StepIntoReading.com
randomhousekids.com

Educators and librarians, for a variety of teaching tools, visit us at RHTeachersLibrarians.com

ISBN 978-0-7364-3811-7 (trade) — ISBN 978-0-7364-8253-0 (lib. bdg.)
ISBN 978-0-7364-3812-4 (ebook)

Printed in the United States of America   10 9 8 7 6 5 4 3 2 1

DISNEY · PIXAR

COCO

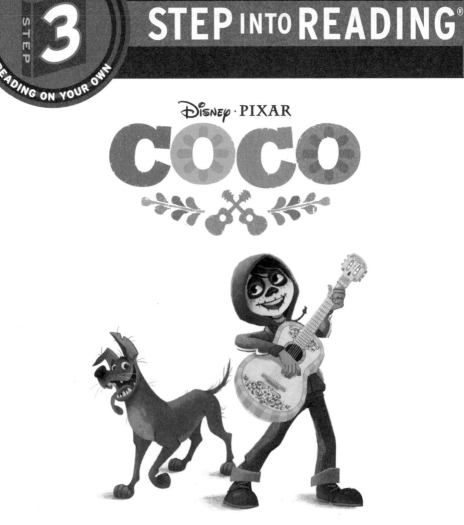

Miguel's Music

adapted by Liz Rivera

illustrated by the Disney Storybook Art Team

Random House 🏠 New York

Hello!

My name is Miguel.

I am twelve years old.

I live in Mexico.

I love music!

I want to be a musician

like Ernesto de la Cruz.

He was once the most popular

singer in Santa Cecilia.

Everyone still loves his music.

Music makes me happy.
But my family doesn't
want me to play it.
In my special hiding place,
I play my guitar in secret.

Only my friend Dante
knows what I do.
He would never tell,
even if he could.
He is a good dog!

Abuelita is my grandma.

She does not like musicians.

Abuelita yells at them.

They are scared of her.

Abuelita does not

like the plaza, either.

But I go there

to see the statue

of Ernesto de la Cruz.

I want to play music

for everyone, just like he did.

When I am not

practicing my music,

I like to spend time

with Mamá Coco.

She is my great-grandma.

She does not talk much.

She is a good listener.

Everyone in my family

makes shoes.

Abuelita says

I must learn

to make shoes

and set up for the holiday.

Every year, we have
Día de los Muertos.
It means "Day of the Dead."
We think about family members
who came before us.

We make a special altar

to honor them.

No one talks about

Mamá Coco's father.

He is the only family member

not included on the altar.

My great-great-grandpa

left the family to play music.

He never came back.

I do not even know his name.

He is why no one

in my family

is allowed to play music.

My family finds out

that I love music.

Abuelita smashes my guitar.

I am so sad.

I find a special guitar.

It belonged to Ernesto de la Cruz!

It is beautiful.

I play a few notes.

Marigolds fly around me!

On Día de los Muertos,
something magical happens.
Dante and I go
to the Land of the Dead!

All my family members
who came before me
are there.
It is amazing.

I meet a musician
named Hector.
We sing together
in front of a lot of people.

It is my favorite silly song.

I dance, too.

The music makes me

jump, spin, and sway.

I see Ernesto de la Cruz!

I am so excited.

I have to sing!

I jump to my feet.

I sing so loudly,

everyone can hear.

Hector gets mad at Ernesto.

Ernesto stole songs

from Hector when they were young.

Ernesto is a bad musician

and a bad friend.

Hector tells me
that he wrote a song
for his daughter, Coco.
That is Mamá Coco's name!
Hector is my great-great-grandpa!

I return to the Land of the Living.
I have to tell Mamá Coco
that Hector always loved her
and wrote a special song for her.

I want Mamá Coco

to remember her father.

I sing the special song.

Mamá Coco remembers it!

We sing the song together.

Everyone is happy!

Now when we remember

our lost loved ones,

we remember

Papá Hector, too.

We play music together

and sing songs,

just like he did.

When I hear my family sing,

I feel their love.

That makes me want

to sing even louder!

I am happy that

music is all around us.